Dear Parent,

The Anne of Green Gables Series was created with the aid of teachers to raise social and educational issues that will benefit young children.

Anne is a strong female character with a colorful vocabulary and a vibrant imagination. Her vocabulary level is meant to stimulate the reading experience for young people. Inserted on the final pages of this book is a handy dictionary for clarification of certain words and expressions.

Step into Anne's world and benefit from her desire to build friendships and inspire others through her wonderful imagination and her determination to succeed!

Log on to **www.learnwithanne.com** and explore an educational guide, with outlines of lesson plans and discussion topics available for teachers and parents alike.

Also check out **www.annetoon.com** for educational games, activities and multimedia that bring Anne's character and friends to life.

Published in 2010 by Davenport Press
110 Davenport Rd.
Toronto, Ontario, M5R 3R3

Printed in Canada

ISBN = 978-0-9736803-7-9

anne of green gables

AS SEEN ON
PBS

Anne's NEW HOME

KEVIN **SULLIVAN** &
ELIZABETH **MORGAN**

Anne Shirley had no parents.
She lived in a horrible orphanage
because there was not a single family
in the whole world who would care for her.

Then Anne got lucky. The orphanage decided to send her to live with Marilla and Matthew, on a farm called Green Gables

When she arrived, Marilla knew someone had made a mistake. She and Matthew, her brother, had asked the orphanage to send them a boy to help do the chores on their farm.

Matthew and Marilla had never had any children of their own. Anne told them she could work as hard as any boy. They took Anne at her word.

Marilla said Anne could stay and live with them at Green Gables.

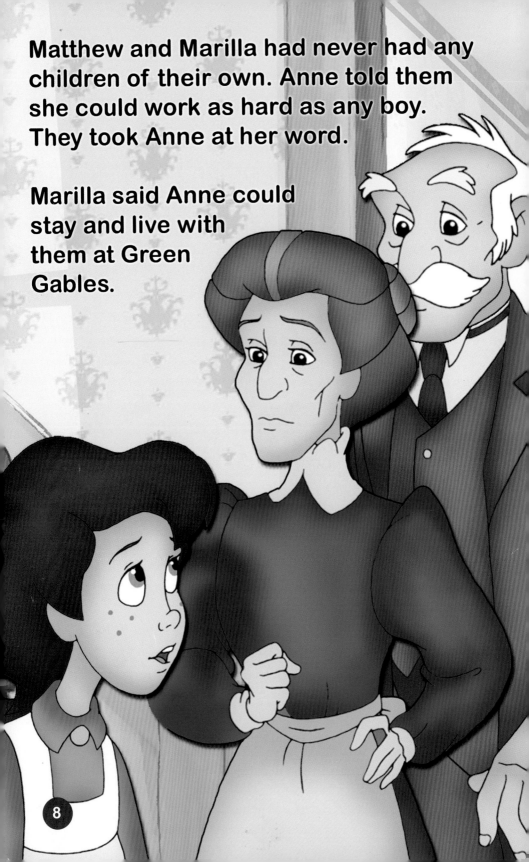

However, she had to go to school,

say her prayers,

do her chores and promise to be obedient. Anne agreed because she wanted to live with people who would love her. 9

Anne really liked school. She made lots of friends. She wanted her friends to like her so she invited them to a party...

... with Marilla's permission, of course. Anne ran to the chicken coop to begin her work.

"Oh Marilla, I have so many chores to do and so little time!"

Anne ran back to the house.
She put her basket of eggs on the
shelf above the woodpile.

Then she went to her room to
make decorations.

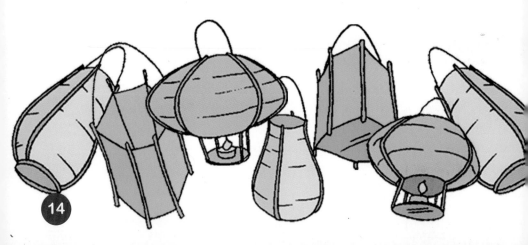

"Anne didn't bring in any wood!"

The next morning Marilla was cooking breakfast. She ran out of wood for the stove.

Marilla went to the woodpile. She bent down to get some wood. Then she stood up. Her head hit the shelf.

"Oww!"

The basket of eggs tumbled onto her. She was a sticky, gooey mess!

"Oh, Marilla! I'm sorry. But I just can't get my chores done until everything is ready for my party."

"Anne Shirley, you can't get your chores done AND have a party too. So the party will have to be cancelled."

"But Marilla! All my friends are coming!"

"You can tell them they can't come. If you are to be part of our family, you must pull all your weight first."

She dreamt that Marilla, Matthew
and she were enjoying a beautiful day.

Anne went to the kitchen. The door
handle came off. Matthew hadn't
fixed it because he was too busy resting.

When Anne woke up,she
knew what she needed to do.

Anne happily finished all her chores. Then Marilla turned to her and told her she could still have her party.

All of Anne's new friends came from school. Marilla served lemonade and cookies. Even Matthew had a good time.

When it was over, Anne told
Marilla how much she really loved her.

Anne's Fancy Dancy Words

Chores - tasks and jobs to do around the house

Duties - jobs and tasks

Horrible - very bad

Laundry - clothes that need washing or have been washed

Obedient - to follow orders

Anne's Fancy Dancy Words

Orphanage - a place for children who do not have parents

Permission - when someone allows you to do something

Prepare - to get ready

Tumble - fell down

Wandered - to drift or go in another direction